THE BLESSING NISSER

Published by: Nisser World Publishing Company

www.blessingnisser.com

Illustrated by: Diane Knesovich - www.dianek.net

Photography, Interior and Cover Design by: Marion Pinto-Borges

ISBN: 978-0-9991296-0-9

Printed in China

The Blessing Nisser

An Advent Journey of Kindness through Denmark

KIRSTIE MARX

To Ingrid, who was my first example of what it meant to bless and serve those around you

To my girls, you both fill my heart with love, joy, and laughter and you know how to be a blessing to others

For Rich, you are my strength and my comfort, you encourage me to soar

This book is for you Lord, it is yours

Foreword

Growing up in Denmark from the age of eight to fifteen was a perfect way to spend a childhood. I was raised in a small town in southern Denmark where community and relationships were important. We biked to school through rain, wind or snow. Christmas time was magical. The darkness outside didn't bother us as we gathered around the table with candles glowing and spent time with one another. The Christmas season included outings to the forests to gather greenery, visits to the special Christmas markets and sampling the wonderful special foods.

For many years, I've wanted to write a book about the Blessing Nisser. They have visited our own home in North Carolina for several years. My husband and I desired for our two daughters to truly understand what Christmas is about: the birth of Jesus and loving and serving others. In order to help us accomplish this, we added the Blessing Nisser to our holiday traditions.

A Nisse in Denmark is a mythical character that lives in the rafters of a barn. They are temperamental and need to be fed rice pudding in order to behave. I chose to make my Nisser into Blessing Nisser. They bring the community and families together by serving and loving others. I have taken liberty to have the Blessing Nisser in the story kind and caring, not temperamental. Our view of the Blessing Nisser is our own. In the kit, you will find items to make your own Nisser. Every picture I have seen of the Nisser portray them with a tall, red hat. I would encourage you to buy felt and other fabric and let your children make the Nisser into their own. You will have fond memories looking back years later on their personal creations.

This book can be read all at once or daily in December. In our home, we read the whole story after Thanksgiving. Then my husband and I look through the provided cards to come up with what service projects we want to do. We intend to do one every day of the month. However, you may decide to just do them on Monday, Wednesday and Friday or on the weekends. That is the beauty of this book, it is up to you. We have also provided you with blank cards that you can fill in with your own ideas and traditions. In addition, we have included cards that say "you have been loved by the Blessing Nisser." If you need more than what was provided, you can order additional cards from the website. www.blessingnisser.com

Our family's prayer, is that you will be blessed hearing about the love of Jesus and how Charlotte and the Nisser reflect Him through serving and loving others. We pray this book will become a tradition in your family for many years to come. When I finished reading this story to my youngest daughter, she hurried upstairs and made our bed and left a note on our pillow, saying "you have been loved by the Blessing Nisser"--all unbeknownst to us. Just by hearing the story, she wanted to bless us. Our prayer is that children will be inspired to love and serve others. Please post your stories to the Facebook page, sharing about how the Blessing Nisser came to your home.

Kirstie Marx

It was one of those frosty days in early winter when you just want to snuggle under a blanket, drink hot tea, and watch the birds and squirrels prepare for the bitter cold to come. Ellie and I cuddled on our back porch, warm and toasty, as we talked about Christmas, which was just around the corner. She excitedly shared about the family she would see, Christmas presents she hoped to receive, and the special times she anticipated experiencing this December. Then, she asked me what Christmas was like in Denmark, where I spent my childhood.

"What was it like? Did you have snow? Was it cold? Did you get a lot of presents? Remind me what the Blessing Nisser are again, Mama!"

"Blessing Nisser are little helpers who bring the community together and encourage us to serve and bless others during the Christmas season."

The questions flowed, and I chuckled, stepping back in time and recalling the same excitement I felt many years ago as a child anticipating the Christmas season...

Growing up in Denmark, I, Charlotte vividly remember the cold, dark days of winter. My family, the Olsen's, consisted of my two older brothers, Frederik and Hans, and my younger sister Helena. We lived on a farm with white-washed walls and a red tin roof that pitter pattered when it rained. Frederik had a great deal of responsibility on the farm, which carried over into his studies. Hans and I were close in age, but Hans was the mischievous one. Then there was Helena, the baby of the family, who was just sweet enough to be annoying. Christmas was a special time in our home, filled with delectable smells, the ringing of bells, candles all over the house, mountains of presents, and the Blessing Nisser.

We snuggled closer and to Denmark we went, more than 4000 miles away many, many years ago…

It is November 28th, and I awoke with a start. Is today the day the Blessing Nisser will arrive? I lean over and glance at the calendar near my bed. Still two days to go. I eagerly await the arrival of the Blessing Nisser every year. They live out in the rafters of our barn. Every morning I tip-toe out there to give them a bowl of rice pudding with a slather of butter and pinch of cinnamon on top. When I come back the next morning, the bowl is always empty. I wonder what we will do this year and if this is the year that Hans will be able to see them. The Nisser don't show themselves unless you understand what love means. Even though Hans said he saw them last year, I highly doubt it. The Blessing Nisser help gather the community together and encourage them to serve one another. However, I haven't seen Hans serve anyone or Mr. Anderson, the grumpy old man up the street. Mr. Anderson is all alone; someone said his wife died years ago and his son moved to America. Could this be the year the Blessing Nisser touch their hearts?

Rasmus and Ingrid creep along the rafters with their noses pointed up high.

"What is that delicious smell?" Rasmus asks.

"I think-oh, how I hope it is rice pudding!" Ingrid laughs out loud.

"It can only mean one thing..." they say in unison, "It is almost Christmas time!"

They traveled all year long and recently moved back under the rafters.

"Quick! Get the spoons," Rasmus yells.

Within a minute, they both bow their heads and thank the good Lord for his provision. The butter has melted and the cinnamon has spread throughout all the nooks and crannies of the pudding. Their lips smack together.

"The first bite is always the best bite!" Ingrid exclaims.

As they sit close together enjoying the delectable treat, their thoughts quickly turn to the meaning of the Christmas season. It is about a little baby born in a manger and how He grew up to serve others and to one day save them. Both Rasmus and Ingrid know they have a job to do and they eagerly set out to do it. Their task is to remind everyone why they celebrate Christmas and to show people how to love and serve one another. Rasmus and Ingrid pray that this year will be the year that Mr. Anderson and Hans will understand how much they are loved.

"All right, Ingrid," Rasmus says, "What is the plan this year?"

She jumps up from the table to gather all her supplies. Joy shines out of her eyes. Ingrid's favorite part of making plans is thinking up ideas and wondering who they can help this year. She remembers people from the past who changed because they finally understood what it meant to love. At the top of the piece of paper, she writes "Mr. Anderson and Hans" in big, bold letters.

"This is going to be a very hard year, Rasmus," she says sadly. "Mr. Anderson is hurting so much from being lonely and all Hans can think about is himself."

"I know," Rasmus replies, "but they probably need help more than anyone else in the village, don't you think?"

"Mr. Anderson and Hans have no idea what is coming their way this year, do they, Ingrid?"

"No!" she chuckles, "Oh, what fun it will be. Do you think we can have Charlotte assist us? We can give her tasks to do everyday to show love. Is it too dangerous? You know, we cannot appear in front of the people until they understand what love means, Rasmus."

Rasmus sits up a little taller and proclaims, "Of course we can do this. All we have to do is show them what it means to love and serve."

Ingrid and Rasmus sit for what seems like hours trying to come up with different tasks for Charlotte to complete.

- Do your siblings' chores
- Compliment at least five people today
- Leave a sweet treat for the postman
- Donate food to a homeless shelter
- Go Christmas caroling

Ideas tumble out of the excited Nisser. Finally, they both stretch to release the tension from their backs. They had been hunched over the list for quite some time.

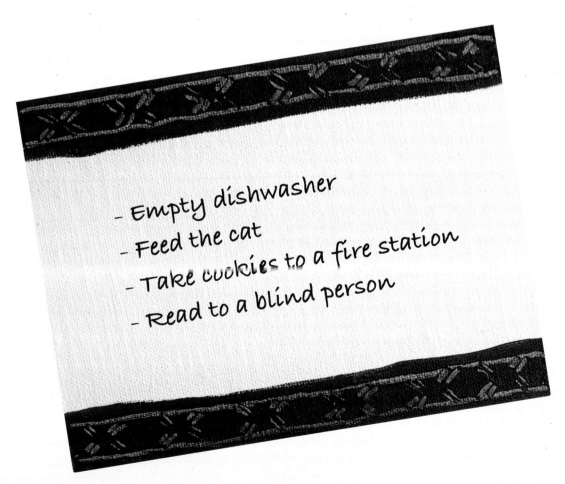

- Empty dishwasher
- Feed the cat
- Take cookies to a fire station
- Read to a blind person

"Ugh, November 30th is not my favorite time of the year. Just bring me Christmas morning and all the presents," Hans moans as he lays in bed looking out the window. "It is 7:30 and it is still dark outside. "I'm tired of biking to the school in the dark, sitting in class while it is light outside, and then biking back home again in the dark. Not fair. I want to live where it is warm and sunny, not cold, freezing Denmark!" moans Hans as he walks into the kitchen. Charlotte is standing by the sink with a big smile and she looks expectantly at Hans.

"What do you want?" he grumbles.

"Nothing!" she smiles and sits down for breakfast with a knowing look on her face. "Hans, it is almost December 1st, my favorite time of the year. I love baking, making decorations, caroling around the village, and looking for the Blessing Nisser!" Charlotte says in a sing-song voice.

"Bah Humbug!" Hans retorts. "You keep talking about the Blessing Nisser, Charlotte, but I don't believe in them and I am tired of you talking about them."

"Oh Hans, you are so grumpy and selfish, you couldn't see them even if you tried."

"I have seen them!" he sneers, trying to act all grown up.

Hans' unkindness makes Charlotte doubt what he says. However, she prays this will be the year where he does see them. She finishes her breakfast in silent pondering and hurries out to the barn where she knows she will see Rasmus and Ingrid.

Hello, Charlotte! Did you bring us rice pudding?" Rasmus asks expectantly.

"Of course I did! Over there on the table."

Ingrid gives Charlotte a huge hug and tells her how much she missed her over the past year. They talk for a few minutes before Charlotte asks who they plan to bless this year.

"We think we should bless Mr. Anderson and Hans," Rasmus says. Ingrid and I have come up with some tasks for you to do which will show Mr. Anderson and Hans that you love them. You will teach them, through serving with a willing heart, to show love. Every day you will find a note with your task for the day. Once you are finished, you will leave Mr. Anderson or Hans a note saying, **"You have been loved by the Blessing Nisser."** That way the focus is not on you. Charlotte, you understand what it means to serve and love another. That is why we are asking for your help."

On **December 1st** Charlotte wakes up with the following note on her pillow: "Here is the countdown candle and some clay. Gather greenery from the garden and bless your parents with a beautiful arrangement."

Charlotte knew Rasmus snuck into her room during the night to leave the note. She runs to Helena's bedroom to show her the note, and Helena jumps up in excitement because she wants to help her big sister.

"Charlotte, what is a countdown candle?" asks Helena innocently.

"A countdown candle is a candle with the numbers 1-24 on the side of it to represent the days before Christmas!! Every night in December, we light the candle and let it burn down one number to remind ourselves when Christmas is coming," Charlotte replies.

One of Helena and Charlotte's favorite things to do at Christmas time is to gather greenery from the woods to decorate and make the house smell like Christmas. Rasmus knows how Charlotte loves blessing her parents with gifts from the great outdoors. To top the gift of greenery off, Helena and Charlotte sit down and write a notecard to their parents together which says, "You have been loved by the Blessing Nisser."

On **December 2ⁿᵈ** Charlotte's task for the day is to make cards for the soldiers in the military to bless them for Christmas since they can't spend it with their families. December 2nd is also the first day of Advent. "Advent" means "coming" in Latin, and Charlotte loves celebrating Advent with her family. For the four Sundays before Christmas, the Olsen family gathers together in the evening and lights a candle on the Advent wreath as well as the Christmas candle. From the greenery that Charlotte and Helena gathered, the children make an Advent wreath out of evergreen leaves and attach four candles to the leaves. Another family tradition during Advent is to make *aebleskiver* (little round pastries), drink *Gløgg* (a sweet grape drink), and read about the coming of baby Jesus in the manger.

Rasmus and Ingrid decide that in order to show Mr. Anderson and Hans what love means, they will bless both of them several times leading up to Christmas. However, their job is also to bless the rest of the village. During the night of **December 3ʳᵈ** when everyone else in the village is asleep, the two Blessing Nisser scurry around the village leaving minty candy canes on everyone's doorsteps. Once again, they leave a note saying, "You have been loved by the Blessing Nisser."

"Can you imagine everyone's surprise when they wake up, Rasmus?" Ingrid laughs.

December 4th is Frederik's birthday. Charlotte and Helena wake up extra early to make him pancakes for his special day. In Denmark there is a word called *hygge* which means to gather with friends and family and enjoying the cozy atmosphere created with candles, music, and people you love. It is also the feeling you get when your house is full of family and friends during Christmas and you are making memories. Charlotte and Helena pull out a tray, add a little greenery, light a candle, and carry the pancakes into the kitchen while singing happy birthday to Frederik. Birthdays are a special time to celebrate, and the girls try to fill Frederik's day with blessings.

Later that day, Charlotte comes skipping and laughing into the barn.

"What is it, my dear?" Ingrid inquires.

Charlotte jumps from one leg to the other, smiling from ear to ear. She can't contain herself much longer.

"I am about to burst," she says. "I bet you can't guess my good news!"

"We give up - what is it?" Rasmus and Ingrid laugh.

"We are going to go to Copenhagen in 10 days to see our cousins. I've never been to Copenhagen at Christmas time, and I can't wait to see the palace all decorated and walk down *Strøget*, which is the longest pedestrian shopping street in all of Europe. I have even heard there are Christmas markets on every single corner. I am so excited!" Charlotte blurts out, trying to catch her breath.

Ingrid and Rasmus turn to look at each other, the same thought floating through their minds. How fun would a couple of days in Copenhagen be!

"May we go with you, Charlotte?" they plead.

Charlotte hesitates for a moment, pondering the question and wondering if it could be possible to hide them in her suitcase. It might help bless Hans.

"Absolutely!" she squeals. "Hans would never expect you to bless him in Copenhagen! It is only ten days away, which means we have a lot of preparation ahead of us. The Nisser grin from ear to ear and rush to give Charlotte a hug. Charlotte skips all the way home, while the two Nisser put their heads together and start making plans.

As long as Charlotte can remember (which isn't very long), Mr. Anderson has been a grumpy old man. His wife died before Charlotte was born, and every time she sees him, the gruff, elderly neighbor is muttering under his breath.

"I wonder how I can bless him this year so he understands what love is," Charlotte wonders. "Maybe I can rake his leaves, wash his windows, or bake him something special. I will start off small and then shower him with blessings."

Walking home from school the next day, which is **December 5th**, Charlotte picks some evergreens and a few twigs dotted with berries. She ties a red ribbon around them with another note from the Nisser and places the gift upon Mr. Anderson's front step. Charlotte doesn't dare stick around to see if Mr. Anderson appreciates her gift. She remembers what Ingrid tells her, "You are not blessing them so you can be recognized: you are blessing them so they can see the love in you." She glances over her shoulder and runs back home to spend time with her family by candlelight.

December 6th is St. Nicholas Day so Ingrid and Rasmus bless all the children in the Olsen house with some sweet treats in their shoes, which the children had set outside the night before. Hans has been observing Charlotte over the past couple of days.

"Why is she always so happy and joyful," he thinks, "while I am always down? I will have to watch her carefully to see if I can find out her secret. She must have some reason to do all these things for other people." Hans truly doesn't understand why Charlotte is blessing others!

The people who handle the post all around the world are especially busy during the month of December. Today is **December 7th** and it is Charlotte's task to bless the postman. She takes out her colored pencils and draws him a pretty picture of herself along with two funny looking characters. One of them has a long, grey beard and wears a red hat.The other has big, rosy cheeks and a scarf around her neck. Charlotte leaves the picture along with some homemade cinnamon cookies in the mailbox. She attaches a note which says, "You have been loved by the Blessing Nisser."

December 8th's note reads: "Look through your toys and give five items away."

Charlotte sits on her bed in deep thought for a minute, then runs to share the note with Hans. He just laughs at her kindness and belief in the Nisser.

"Really Charlotte, why would you ever want to give your toys away? They belong to you. Mum and Dad bought them for you."

"There are children out there who don't have even one toy and I have tons," she rebukes.

Charlotte silently sorts through her toy box with a heavy heart after Hans's comments, but nevertheless she finds eleven toys to donate. Hans hides behind the door and peeks through the crack to watch Charlotte, his face painted with surprise.

"There is no way I will give any of my toys away," he thinks, "because they are all mine!" However, later that day as he cleans his room, he picks up two toys.

"These silly toys are not worth keeping, so I'll sneak them into Charlotte's box. She'll never even notice."

Little does Hans know, but Rasmus stands hidden in the corner, witnessing the whole thing. Rasmus wonders if Hans' heart is softening because he is seeing the love in Charlotte's heart.

December 9th is the second Sunday in Advent. Charlotte wakes up with a yawn and stretches from head to toe. She finds no note from Rasmus or Ingrid so she decides to bless them today. She makes them a miniature advent wreath because she notices their home in the rafters is quite bare. She creeps up the wooden stairs, trying to avoid the squeaky parts, and leaves the Advent wreath and some *æbleskiver* on the table with a note that says, "You have been loved by me." Why not be a blessing to the Blessing Nisser?

Today is one of Charlotte's favorite days of the school year. On **December 10th**, although the children still bike to school, they don't have to do schoolwork. Instead, they make traditional Danish Christmas decorations. In her class, the teacher arranges tons of colored paper, glue, scissors, glitter, and fresh greenery to spur everyone's creativity. Charlotte loves making *julehjerter* which are woven Christmas hearts. People hang these traditional crafts from the Christmas tree and in windows and give them away as gifts. She also loves making Danish christmas stars but they are much harder and more time consuming to create. With a little perseverance and nimble fingers she is able to make four. Her note for today says "Hug a friend," so Charlotte runs up to her teacher and gives her a gentle hug.

Charlotte wakes up the next day thinking about Mr. Anderson. Does he like Christmas? Does he have any decorations? Who sings him Christmas carols? Today is **December 11th**, almost halfway to Christmas! She decides to share some of the decorations that she made yesterday at school with Mr. Anderson to brighten up his home. She carefully wraps up four *julehjerter* and one of her cherished Christmas stars and ties the package with a pretty red ribbon, just like the one she used for the greenery. As she runs out of the house, Charlotte remembers that she forgot to attach the note!! She wants Mr. Anderson to know he is loved, so she rushes back to her room and grabs the note. Running to Mr. Anderson's home, Charlotte leaves the package on his doorstep and dashes all the way home without looking back. A gleam shines in her eye and a smile dances across her face.

Ingrid and Rasmus sometimes do chores for the people in the village. It is common knowledge among the Danes that you have to treat the Nisser kindly and feed them rice pudding or they may cause trouble. Before the rooster crows his early morning wake-up call, Ingrid and Rasmus are discussing whose chores they will complete.

"Ingrid, today is **December 12th** and we haven't seen much of Hans. Last week I saw him give two of his toys away without anyone noticing!" Rasmus exclaims. "How about we bless him today and feed the chickens and dogs for him?"

"Excellent idea, Rasmus! Let me write him a note. I wonder if he will be surprised!" Ingrid agrees.

A few hours later a sleepy, weary Hans drags his tired body through the door in the barn because he stayed up late watching the national Christmas show on the television. Grumbling to himself, Hans mutters, "Why do I have to feed these animals? Why can't they take care of themselves? It is freezing out here. I can see my breath and would love nothing more than to be warm in bed. I bet there are icicles hanging from the rafters," he shivers as he glances up.

Hans stares a little longer than normal because he sees something move out of the corner of his eye. He shakes off the feeling that someone is watching him and instead turns to feed the chickens.

"That's odd, they are already eating..." Hans walks over to check on the dogs and finds that they are sitting contentedly, licking their chops. They must have been fed, too!

"I wonder who fed the animals for me?" Hans says as he rubs his hand across his chin. He glances at the happy dogs and notices a red ribbon with a note around one of the dog's necks which says, "You have been loved by the Blessing Nisser."

Startled, he jumps, and quickly looks up into the rafters, once again, wondering if someone is watching him. He pokes around the barn for a few minutes but doesn't see anything, so he gathers his hat off the ground, whistles a merry tune, and heads back into the warm house for a hearty breakfast.

"Whew, that was a close one Rasmus!" Ingrid exclaims. "Do you think he saw us?"

"No, we were very lucky this time. We will have to be more careful in the future. I think he might be onto our plan," Rasmus decides.

December 13th is Santa Lucia day in Denmark. A group of young ladies dress up in white, silky dresses and one special girl is chosen to wear a wreath on her head that is adorned with real candles. Charlotte is not chosen to be Santa Lucia this year and she shuffles around the house, disappointment written all over her face. She still gets to be a part of the processional but her heart was set on being Santa Lucia. As she is getting ready to go to the party, she spots a note which says,

"We understand you are disappointed, but the best way to cure a sad heart is to give compliments to others!"

Charlotte sits and wonders how she can compliment others when her heart is so sad.

"Maybe Kristen, who is the Santa Lucia, is nervous. I know I would be nervous if I was the Santa Lucia. Maybe I can commend her on what a great job she is doing!" As the morning wears on, Charlotte is able to complement several people and before she realizes it, her heart is full of joy. She sees how much her kindness means to others. She is able to bless all those around her, just by using her words.

December 14th arrives on a cold, blustery day. The trees sway in the wind and the wind howls a fierce tune. Inside, however, there is quite a different scene to behold. Laughter and anticipation fill the air. Today is the day to go to Copenhagen and see the cousins. During the night, Rasmus and Ingrid sneaked into Charlotte's room where they placed a note on her bed before hiding in her backpack. They promised Charlotte that they would be very quiet and stay out of the way. Rasmus and Ingrid are excited to see the sites by peeking out of the tiny holes in Charlotte's backpack, but intend to be as quiet as a mouse.

All the children jump in the car and the family is off!

"To the train station we go!" yells Helena. They plan on taking the train from southern Denmark across Fyn before going over one of the largest free-standing bridges in the world, The *Storebælt Bridge*. Charlotte has warned the Nisser to stay low because she doesn't want them to be frightened.

Right after lunch, the family arrives and hears the bustling sounds of Copenhagen. Their cousins, Søren and Ulla are anxiously awaiting their arrival.

"We have a whole afternoon planned out for you!" Ulla exclaims. First, we are going to *Vor Frelsers Kirke*, which is about one mile from here. From there, you can hike up 400 steps and get the best view of the city. After that, we are going to walk on *Strøget* and we will have a red hotdog and go shopping.

Doesn't that sound wonderful?"

All the children agree that it does. Frederik is very excited to go up the 400 steps and see the city. Earlier that day Charlotte saw the note from Rasmus and Ingrid. "Find someone in need and bless them today." She tucks the note in her winter coat and sets out to find that special someone.

Rasmus isn't feeling too well. Being in Charlotte's backpack as she circles up Vor Frelsers Kirke leaves his tummy quite unsettled. The bridge did not help matters for him.

"Shh, Rasmus," whispers Ingrid, "you can't moan or be sick. We don't want anyone to see or hear you!"

"But, my tummy hurts. Are we almost to the top?" Rasmus moans. A few minutes later Rasmus takes a deep breath. Charlotte had reached the top where the air is cool and refreshing.

"Whew, that was a close one. Do you think I can pull the zipper back and stick my head out, Ingrid? I just want to see the sites and try to spot the Little Mermaid. I have read so many books by Hans Christian Andersen, and do you remember the one about the Little Mermaid?"

"Be very careful, Rasmus," Ingrid scolds. Rasmus slowly pulls the zipper back one inch at a time, lifting his head to peak out.

"Wow, Ingrid! I can see all of Copenhagen from up here. Look over there at the barges on the water. Over here you can see *Rundetårn*. I love all the red roofs and colorful buildings!" Rasmus shouts. Suddenly, the hairs on Rasmus' neck stand up, he gets a tingling feeling down his back, and he begins to feel as if someone is watching him. But who? He quickly crouches down and pulls Ingrid with him.

"I think Hans saw me," he stammers. "Where can we hide?" Ingrid clearly sees how frightened Rasmus is. The two sit quietly and try not to move.

"Charlotte, what is in your backpack?" Hans asks.

"Oh nothing much, just some books and left over candy. Would you like one?" Charlotte asks with a look of innocence.

"Is that all you have in there?"

"Well, I do have some other things in there, but nothing worth looking at," she says as she holds up a piece of candy. Charlotte knows she needs to distract Hans or he will look in her bag. Thankfully, the candy is enough of a diversion. The Blessing Nisser are safe.

"Whew!" they both say in unison, "We better stay down low."

The Olsen children and their cousins tour the Rundetårn, walk on *Strøget*, and eat a red hotdog.

"We have saved the best for last," Søren tells the group. "Copenhagen is famous for their Christmas markets and tonight we will go." All the children are thrilled. They have heard about the markets for many years but have never gone. Charlotte is looking forward to shopping, Helena is looking forward to seeing all the crafts, Frederik wants to get some Gløgg, and Hans is thinking about filling his belly. There will be many delicious treats to enjoy! Rasmus and Ingrid hope to find some rice pudding, too.

The Christmas market is on *Strøget*. It looks like a scene from Greenland. Little wooden huts line both sides of the street. Snow coats the rooftops. The lights twinkle in the light breeze while Christmas carolers sing by the magnificent fire in the middle of the square. From one direction drifts the aroma of nuts cooked with cinnamon spices, from the opposite, rice pudding and hot dogs. The children are giddy with excitement as Father hands them each some money and tells them to meet back in an hour. The big boys are to watch over Helena.

Charlotte knows she wants to buy a few Christmas presents as well as try some rice pudding. Ulla puts her arm through Charlotte's and the two cousins are off. First, they find a book for Father. Next, a little angel for Helena. Charlotte spots some bright, red wooly mittens.

"Oh, these would be perfect for me!" she exclaims.

Charlotte pays the kind lady and off the girls go to get their rice pudding.

"Would you ladies like butter and cinnamon?" the server inquires when the girls place their orders.

"Yes, please!" they both laugh. "The cinnamon and butter are the best part!"

Charlotte remembers Rasmus and Ingrid in her backpack. She leaves a bit of rice pudding in the cup, closes the lid, and places it in her backpack. The next moment she hears a "Hurrah" coming from the backpack. Charlotte smiles to herself because she knows Rasmus and Ingrid are enjoying their special treat.

As the children walk back towards their cousins' house, they see an old man lying down on a bench in the park.

"Who is that?" Helena asks.

"That is Mr. Vestergård. He doesn't have a home so he sleeps in the park," Søren said.

"He looks kind of scary to me," Helena whispers.

"Oh no, Mr. Vestergård is a very kind man. A few weeks ago I had a flat tire, and he helped me carry my bike all the way home," Søren says proudly. "He is my friend. Let me introduce you to him."

The children walk over to meet Mr. Vestergård. He is a friendly, old man. Charlotte notices that he doesn't have any mittens despite the freezing weather. She remembers the beautiful, woolen pair she just bought. Did the Blessing Nisser want her to bless Mr. Vestergård? After a friendly chat, the children say their goodbyes and begin walking away. But before they've gone far, Charlotte turns and darts back to Mr. Vestergård. She takes out the bag holding the mittens and hands them to him. Charlotte quietly watches as Mr. Vestergård opens the bag. She sees tears glistening in the elderly man's eyes before hearing his words, "Sweet, young lady, I have been praying for a new pair of mittens. You see, the other day I met a lady with a baby. She was pushing a stroller and she didn't have any mittens on. I knew I had to give her mine and trusted the good Lord would provide. Today, He did that through you. Thank you, my dear."

Charlotte feels warm all over. She reaches in her bag and pulls out a note that says, "You have been loved by the Blessing Nisser." She hands Mr.

Vestergård the note, wraps him in a hug, and runs to join the other children. Hans witnesses the entire exchange, and once again wonders about the source of the joy radiating from his sister.

The children wake up early, eagerly wondering what **December 15th** will hold. They know they will be able to play this morning with their cousins and tour the city a little more later on in the day. They eat breakfast, get dressed, and begin to play, eager with anticipation at the surprise their parents say is in store.

Amalienborg is where the royal family lives. There are four impressive, cream colored buildings all facing each other with a large courtyard in the middle. As the children approach the Palace, Charlotte and Helena gasp in delight.

"It is so beautiful! Do you see all those windows? Look at the large Christmas tree. I can't believe we are able to walk this close to where the royal family lives," Charlotte says breathlessly.

"They even have *julehjerter* in the windows just like we do," Helena says in a proud voice.

Søren tells the children that the royal family are part of the people of Denmark. They are often seen walking the streets just like ordinary people. The Danes love their royal family and the children are so excited to see where they live.

Next the children travel to Tivoli, the second oldest amusement park in the world. It opened in 1843 and takes up several blocks in downtown Copenhagen. People come from all over the world to go to Tivoli. The children learn that tonight, they will visit Tivoli as their surprise!

"Rasmus! Wake up! Did you hear that? We are going to Tivoli tonight!" exclaims Ingrid.

Rasmus leaps up. "Tivoli you say? Are we really going to Tivoli?"

"Yep! There are rides everywhere. There is even a wooden roller coaster that is more than 100 years old. I can't wait to see all the twinkling lights in the trees, the boats on the water, and the pantomime show," Ingrid says dreamily.

"Forget all of that, Ingrid, what about all the food?" Rasmus exclaims. "It is all about the food and the roller coasters for me."

"We had better make sure to be as quiet as mice, so we don't surprise Hans again. I think he is seeing the love in Charlotte and is wondering why she serves and loves others. We need to think of one more thing that may show him," says Ingrid.

"Let's leave a note for Charlotte! It can say, "Today serve Hans by letting him go first in line, letting him choose activities to do, and giving him encouragement!"

The last few days have passed quickly, and today is **December 16th**. Less than ten days until Christmas.

"What a wonderful time we have had in Copenhagen!" the two Nisser exclaim. We will need to hide soon because the family will be leaving."

"Wait a minute, Rasmus. I have to finish my note to Charlotte." Ingrid mutters as she writes, "Today we want you to bless others by leaving encouraging notes wherever you go." "This is going to be a fun one to watch!" Ingrid thinks out loud. "I can't wait to see how creative Charlotte will be."

An hour later, after lots of hugs and tears, Charlotte gathers her things together to go in the car. She sees the note Ingrid left her, smiles, and takes out her sticky notes. She knows she wants to leave a note for her cousin, Ulla.

"You are beautiful inside and out," she writes, sticking the note on Ulla's pillow. Later that day, they stop for dinner. Charlotte takes out her sticky notes, writing, "You are loved." She places the note on the bathroom mirror at the restaurant.

It's **December 17th**, and today Charlotte, Helena, and their Mum are serving their neighbor as a team! They volunteered to babysit for the children while Mr. and Mrs. Hansen go Christmas shopping. The look of gratitude in Mrs. Hansen's eyes when she dropped the children off warmed Charlotte's heart. It truly is better to give than to receive Charlotte thinks, bouncing the giggling baby on her hip.

Last week, Helena saw her sister Charlotte give away some of her toys, so today **December 18th**, Helena decides to give some of her toys away also. The girls gather their old stuffed animals and take them to the police station. The officer is touched by their generosity and praises the girls,

"Now we can pass these on to other children to love. Thank you, girls."

Helena beams. She has seen what her big sister did for others and today, she got to do it, too. It feels so good to bless others.

December 19th is the day Mother has set aside for baking. All the children gather around the kitchen table, even Frederik. Hans wants to make Pebbernødder, which are tiny, little cookies that taste deliciously sweet. Charlotte wants to make *Havregryns Kugler* because she only gets to enjoy them at Christmas time. To make *Havregryns Kugler* you mix butter, oatmeal, confectioner's sugar, and cocoa in a bowl and then roll it into little balls. Then, they get rolled in coconut and stored in the refrigerator. Frederik wants to make marzipan candy and Helena chooses *Vanille Kranse*. For the next three hours, flour flies through the air, laughter echoes through the house, and as the evening draws to a close, an assortment of goodies are left on the kitchen table.

Charlotte and her siblings did not grow up with grandparents; they all passed away. Ingrid knows the children love going to the retirement center to visit. She suggests that they encourage all four of the children to go to the retirement center and read stories with the people there, as well as taking along a basket of baked goods.

"I think that is a great idea, Ingrid!" replies Rasmus.

And so, the note on **December 20**th asks Charlotte to get Frederik, Hans, and Helena, and walk to the retirement center and spend time with the residents.

On the way home from the retirement center, all the children are happy and in a wonderful Christmas mood. They loved reading to the elderly residents, and secretly, the children loved all the treats that were sneaked their way.

"What do you think about old man Mr. Anderson?" Hans asks his siblings as they walk merrily through the chilly air. "Do you think he will move into the retirement home or continue to live on his own?"

Frederik informs the group that he heard some news about it while in the village. Some people mentioned that Mr. Anderson's son is coming home for Christmas and the surprise is that he is bringing his family from America with him. At this, the children stare at one another with excitement, imagining what it would be like to have visitors from America!

The siblings amble closer to their house, when Hans suddenly comes to an abrupt stop, blurting out, "You know what guys? Mr. Anderson's yard is in disarray, a mess and his son is coming home. How about we go tomorrow and clean up his yard for him?"

"Hans, are you sure?" Charlotte asks. She is thrilled to see Hans thinking of someone else for a change.

"Yes, I am sure."

On the morning of **December 21**st all the children awake early, finish their chores and hurry through breakfast. They have a plan for the day and as they open the door to leave, Frederik finds a note taped to the front door. Please bless Mr. Anderson today by cleaning his yard, showing him love. From the Blessing Nisser.

"No way!" the children shout in unison. "How do they know about our plans?"

The siblings step out into a howling, northern wind. The sky is dreary and it feels like snow is in the air.

"Could we have a white Christmas?" Helena asks. Charlotte doesn't know the answer, but she hopes the weather won't interfere with their plans. The boys gather all their tools from the shed out back, the girls gather some cookies and hot chocolate, and the four set out. There are bushes to be chopped back, branches to pick up, windows to be washed, and firewood to be cut. All four children work hard for several hours without complaint. Suddenly, the front door opens and grumpy old Mr. Anderson yells, "What are you doing in my yard?"

Hans steps forward quaking in his boots, yet appearing so mature for his age. He replies, "Mr. Anderson, we want to pass on a Christmas blessing to you by helping clean your yard."

"I don't need any help," roars the surprised homeowner. "If I wanted my yard done I would have done it myself. Now, get off my property."

All four children hurry to gather their tools and cookies, close the gate, and run all the way home. Once safe inside, Helena burst into tears.

"Why was he so mean to us? Doesn't he know we were trying to bless him?"

Charlotte pulls her sister into her arms and squeezes her tight. "Sometimes people don't know how to receive blessings from others," she explains. "We still need to keep blessing Mr. Anderson and maybe soon he will understand that he is loved." Hans takes his sister's comments to heart, turning them over in his head again and again.

Ingrid jumps out of bed in a hurry. Today is **December 22nd**, only two more days until Christmas Eve.

"Rasmus, wake up! We have a lot to do today! Let me look at my list."

Ingrid sets off searching for her list. She soon returns, muttering, "Today we have Christmas caroling in the village, tomorrow is the village Christmas party, and then it is Christmas Eve."

"Two days you say? That isn't a lot of time. Do you think Hans or Mr. Anderson are seeing all the blessings around them yet?" Rasmus yawns loudly, stretching like a cat.

They quickly write out a note for Charlotte. "Bless those around you with your beautiful voice by Christmas caroling!"

Later in the day, Frederik, Hans, Charlotte, and Helena join the other children in the village to sing carols. They knock on various doors and start singing, as the people inside the house join in, passing out cookies and hot chocolate. The last house on the street is Mr. Anderson's. Frederik wants to go and sing, but the other children are not as sure. They discuss the situation a bit, still unsure what to do. Suddenly, Hans marches up and rings Mr. Anderson's doorbell. The children begin singing and a lovely chorus fills the brisk air. Mr. Anderson peaks out his window, then pulls the curtain closed. The singing falters and the children look at one another.

"Maybe Mr. Anderson doesn't like carols after all," Helena says sadly.

Charlotte reminds the others, "Even when people are grumpy and unlovable, that is the time when they need love the most. We shouldn't give up on him."

December 23rd arrives and the children of the village are in a frenzy of excitement!. Today is the annual village Christmas party. The preparations are well under way. The village men arose early to hike into the woods and cut down the enormous tree that will be decorated in the village. Each family will bring homemade decorations and cookies to share. There will be *Gløgg* and hot chocolate to keep everyone warm.

The weather is getting colder; someone even mentions they saw a snowflake or two that morning. No one worries about the weather because they know how special today is going to be. The men set up tables around the corners of the village square. Craft tables overflow with greenery, candles, and clay. Other tables are loaded with paper to make Christmas stars and julehjerter. Cakes, cookies, sweets, and of course marzipan delights are laid out with care. The children continually pass by, trying to get a sneak peek at what they will pick out later. Frederik, Hans, Charlotte, and Helena sit patiently at their table waiting for the mayor to finish up his announcements. Finally, he is done. The children run to get their treats, make the crafts, and meet up with friends. Everyone from the village is there, even old, grumpy Mr. Anderson.

Suddenly, an unexpected car pulls up. A hush falls over the crowd of merrymakers as a question stirs in each person's mind: Is this Mr. Anderson's son? A glance at Mr. Anderson's face tells the villagers the answer; he is smiling from ear to ear! He leaps up, runs to his family, and wraps them in a warm embrace. What a priceless sight to see! The crowd returns to their activities, feeling a bit warmer inside after witnessing the touching family reunion. Frederik, Hans, Charlotte, and Helena are talking joyfully with their friends when Hans notices Mr. Anderson heading to their table. He isn't smiling, and the children move tightly together, bracing themselves for what may come next. However, as he moves closer the children see his face soften. Tears sparkle in Mr. Anderson's eyes as he timidly asks, "Did any of you leave me a bunch of greenery recently? How about some cinnamon cookies?" Charlotte raises her hand gingerly.

"Then I must thank you, my dear," Mr. Anderson says." I know the four of you worked in my garden a few days ago and now I know the reason why. You wanted my yard to look extra nice for my family to see and all I did was yell at you. Would you forgive an old grumpy man? I am so sorry. I have been so lonely and missing my family in America that I totally forgot I have a family right here in the village and that is everyone here. You have taught me what it means to love and serve others, even when someone is as unkind and unloving as I was. You persevered and kept trying. Thank you Charlotte, Frederik, Hans, and Helena. Please come and meet my son and his family. They have just arrived all the way from America."

Charlotte hears some commotion from the Christmas tree. Ingrid and Rasmus, hidden away high in the evergreen, have witnessed the whole exchange. They give each other a high five, nearly tumbling into plain sight.

Later that evening as the family sits around the table enjoying their æbleskiver and telling their parents all about Mr. Anderson and his son, they light the last of the four candles on the Advent wreath. Everyone is happy with how the day has turned out, and the children go to bed without complaining. They know tomorrow will be here soon and they are thrilled!

December 24th is the day when all Danes celebrate Christmas. "Do you think we showed Mr. Anderson and Hans love and served them well? Did we do what we needed to do? Did Charlotte do what she needed to do?" Ingrid was a little worried.

"Ingrid, what are you worrying about? All the Lord asks of us is to show people love and serve them. Do you remember the Bible verse found in Mark 10:45? It says, "For even the Son of Man did not come to be served, but to serve, and give his life as a ransom for many." Jesus showed us many times in the Bible how to serve. We have done all we need to do as has Charlotte. Now we just need to pray and leave a note for Charlotte."

Charlotte slowly woke up from a deep sleep. "Today we celebrate Christmas and there is so much to do. Gather more greenery, cut down the tree, finish wrapping presents, help make the Christmas dinner and hide the almond in the rice pudding. Where to start?" She looks up and notices the note card from the Blessing Nisser.

Well done, Charlotte! You have loved and served well. Today you need to share with Hans about why you love him and were willing to serve him.

Charlotte's heart leaps for joy! She has prayed for this day for so long. She can't wait to talk to Hans, yet she knows it's important to wait until the right time.

The children gather outside to cut down the Christmas tree. Earlier in the year, the family picked out the tree that would stand proudly inside the house. Now, they are ready to chop it down. Each year the children get to take turns cutting the tree. This year it is Charlotte's turn. She eagerly steps up, preparing to take the first swing, when she looks over at Hans and says, "Hans, would you please cut down the tree this year? I really want you to do it."

Hans is speechless. He is still for a few moments, then nods, lifts the axe over his head, and chops down the tree.

"Charlotte, thank you," he says humbly. Cutting the family tree is a great honor, and Hans understands what a sacrifice Charlotte made to bring him joy. Charlotte hugs Hans and walks to the tree. She smiles and asks, "Is anyone going to help me carry this tree?"

Everyone is in a festive mood. The pork roast is cooking in the oven and smells amazing. Tonight the Olsens will enjoy a typical Danish Christmas dinner: pork roast, boiled potatoes, red cabbage, and gravy. Charlotte's favorite is the red cabbage. It is sweet, yet at the same time sour. While the food is cooking, the family gathers to decorate the Christmas tree. They pull out decorations they made and take turns putting them on the tree. Frederik gets to put on the real candles. They are attached to the tree by a little holder that hangs on the branches. After dinner, the candles will be lit and the family will hold hands and circle the tree while singing carols. They don't actually dance, but rather hold hands and circle the tree.

It is time to go to the village church for the Christmas service. Everyone from the village is there. There are candles in all the windows casting a beautiful, soft light. Pastor Larsen steps up into the pulpit and reads from John 3:16, "For God so loved the world, that He gave his only begotten son, that whoever believes in Him, will not perish but have everlasting life."

He continues, "Celebrating Christmas is not about good food and presents. Nor is it about if you have been good or bad. No, it is about love. You see, God loves each one of you. He loves you so much that He sent His only Son to die for you. We are all sinners and we need a Savior. That Savior is Jesus. He was born in a manger even though He deserved so much more. Jesus lived a life free from sin so that He could take our sin and we could be forgiven. If we recognize that we are sinners and that we have a need for a

Savior, and confess with our mouth that Jesus is Lord, then we shall be saved (Romans 10:9-10). Jesus died for us so that we can live in eternity with God. That is what Christmas is about. It is because there was a baby in the manger. We are to love one another and serve each other. Have you done that this Christmas season?"

Hans looks over at Charlotte, and notices the peace on her face. He wonders if this could be the secret his sister has been hiding. She serves everyone around her, even grumpy, old Mr. Anderson! Hans closes his eyes, feeling as if the pastor has been speaking directly to him. For the first time, Hans finally understands what love means. After the service, he walks up to Charlotte, tears shining in his eyes, and hugs her.

"Thank you for loving me even though I was so mean," he begins. "Thank you for serving me and being a wonderful example. You showed me how to give to others and how to put others first. You showed me that even when someone is unlovable you keep loving them. I saw how you served Mr. Anderson and what a difference that made. Charlotte, thank you."

Charlotte hugs Hans in return, who is overcome with thankfulness. She has been faithful to what God called her to and she silently gives Him all the praise and glory. She can hardly wait to tell the Nisser about her good news!

Christmas dinner is always a feast. The table is set with the fine china. Candles gleam in the windows and on the table, reflecting in the glasses. Mother has outdone herself once more. Laughter and joy abound throughout the house. The sound of silverware clinking and sighs of pure bliss reach up to the rafters where earlier in the evening Charlotte set up a Christmas feast for the Blessing Nisser. Rasmus and Ingrid smile when they hear the sweet sounds. They both eagerly anticipate the arrival of their favorite dish--the rice pudding. Every year, Mother puts an almond in the pudding and whoever finds it gets a marzipan pig. Who will get it this year? Frederik, Hans, Charlotte, or Helena?

Silent Night

Silent Night, Holy Night

All is calm, all is bright

Round yon virgin, mother and child

Holy infant so tender and mild

Sleep in heavenly peace,

Sleep in heavenly peace.

After a wonderful meal, everyone exclaims how full they are. Frederik is thrilled at having found the almond and holds the cherished marzipan pig. The children gather around the Christmas tree in awe of its beauty. They love seeing their homemade decorations at the forefront of the tree in the midst of all the gleaming candles. They hold hands and walk around the Christmas tree while raising their voices praising God for His goodness to them.

Helena can't wait any longer; she wants to open up the presents under the tree. Earlier, she spied a gift that looked big enough to hold a new doll. Father passes out one present at a time, so everyone can observe the joy the gift brings.

It is Charlotte's turn to open a beautifully wrapped present with a large bow on top. The tag says it is from Hans. She slowly slides the wrapping paper off and is left speechless. She pulls out a beautiful pair of red mittens, similar to the ones she had given away when she was in Copenhagen. Tears fill her eyes, as she has never been more touched by a gift as she is right now. Hans speaks up and says, "You showed me what it means to love. The moment I saw you give your brand-new mittens away, I knew there was something different about you. Søren and I snuck back the next day to purchase the mittens for you. Merry Christmas, Charlotte! May your hands always be as warm as your heart!"

Rasmus and Ingrid wipe the tears from their small faces. They never grow tired of watching the way hearts transform when people finally understand what it means to love and be loved.

"Well, Rasmus, our job is done!" Ingrid winks at her friend, "No more rice pudding for you until next year!"

"Mama," Ellie snuggles closer, "Thank you for sharing about your childhood Christmas in Denmark. I loved hearing about Mr. Anderson and Hans. Can I serve other people this year, just like you? Will the Blessing Nisser come here this year and leave notes for me?"

I smile down at my precious child, and nod as we gaze at the dancing lights, "I am sure they will my love, I am sure they will."

DENMARK

JYLLAND

FYN

SJÆLLAND

 CHARLOTTE'S HOUSE

 RAILROAD

HANS CHRISTIAN
ANDERSON HOME

 STOREBÆLT BRIDGE

TIVOLI

 COPENHAGEN

44

Havregryns Kugler (Oat balls)
2 1/2 Cup Oatmeal
3/4 Cup Confection Sugar
4 1/2 Tablespoons Cocoa
1 stick butter softened
Finely shredded coconut

Instructions:
Step 1: Mix dry ingredients together in a bowl
Step 2: Add softened butter and mix well
Step 3: Form into 1 inch balls
Step 4: Roll in coconut
Step 5: Can be stored in refrigerator for up to four days

Risengrød (Rice Pudding)
4 people
Preparation time: 40 minutes
Ingredients:
1 cup short-grained white rice (pudding rice)
1/2 cup water
4 1/4 cups milk
1 tsp salt

Cinnamon Sugar
4 tbsp sugar
1 tbsp cinnamon

Instructions:
Step 1: Pour the water and the rice in a large sauce pan. Add salt, heat it up, and let it boil for about 2 minutes.
Step 2: Pour the milk into the pan and boil it while stirring.
Step 3: Let the rice pudding boil lightly for about 35 minutes under a lid. Remember to stir in the pudding regularly so that the rice does not burn to the bottom of the pan.
Step 4: Make some cinnamon sugar by mixing the sugar and cinnamon in a small bowl.

Tip: Serve the rice pudding with a tablespoon of butter and the cinnamon sugar.

Glossary

Amalienborg: home to the Danish Royal Family in the center of Copenhagen. The changing of the guard happens there every day at noon.

Æbleskiver: "Pancake Puffs," traditional pancakes in a distinctive shape of a sphere. The name literally means apple slices in Danish, although apples are not usually an ingredient in present-day versions. Many people today use jam or nutella on top of them.

Blessing Nisser: traditional Danish fairy tale figures that show up at Christmas to help and serve others.

Christmas stars: small handmade stars that are made using thin strips of paper.

Copenhagen: capital of Denmark, located on the island Sjaeland

Countdown candle: Danish families light a candle that has numbers 1-24 written on the side. They burn the candle down one number each day.

Fyn: an island between the mainland Jylland and Sjaeland, where Copenhagen is located.

Gløgg: form of mulled wine, usually made with red wine along with various mulling spices and sometimes raisins. It is served hot or warm and may be alcoholic or non-alcoholic.

Hygge: a warmth of heart, generated from time spent with family or friends. The glow of candles is often used to foster this atmosphere or feeling

Julehjerter: Christmas Hearts are a typical Danish decoration with two pieces of paper or fabric interwoven together.

Little Mermaid: story written by Hans Christian Andersen in 1836. The bronze statue was made to honor the author. It is Denmark's most iconic tourist attraction.

Marzipan pig: awarded to the person who finds an almond in the rice pudding.

Pebbernødder: a sweet spicy cookie traditionally made at Christmas.

Red Hot dogs: a national delicacy in Denmark. They are served on a bun with ketchup, mustard, remoulade, chopped onions, fried onions, and crisp, sweet pickles.

Santa Lucia: a young Christian martyr who died during the Diocletianic Persecution in 304 AD. Throughout Scandinavia, each town elects its own Santa Lucia. This is a girl between the ages of 10-13. The festival begins with a procession led by the Santa Lucia designee, who is followed by young girls dressed in white and wearing lighted wreaths on their heads and boys dressed in white pajama-like costumes singing traditional songs.

Strøget: longest pedestrian shopping center in Europe. It is almost one mile long.

Storebælt Bridge: an 18 km bridge connecting the Western and Eastern parts of Denmark.

Tivioli: the oldest amusement park in Europe. It is famous for its wooden roller coaster. It takes up several blocks in the center of Copenhagen.

Vanille Kranse: Denmark's best known cookie. It is a sugar dough designed as a wreath.

Vor Frelsers Kirke: baroque church in central Copenhagen. It is famous for its helix spire with an external winding staircase that can be climbed to the top, offering extensive views over central Copenhagen.

Julehjerter
(Danish Christmas Hearts)

Designed by Sophia Borges

1. Print this sheet twice and cut out the oval shape on both pieces.

2. Fold in half on the solid line and cut the dotted lines.

3. Weave the folded pieces together.

Tip: Red and white paper look lovely and festive too!

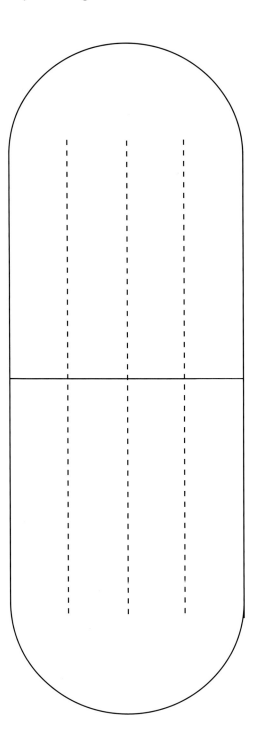